leapfrog

The Nightingale

First published in 2006 by
Franklin Watts
338 Euston Road
London
NW1 3BH

Franklin Watts Australia
Hachette Children's Books
Level 17/207 Kent Street
Sydney
NSW 2000

Text © Anne Cassidy 2006
Illustration © Serena Curmi 2006

A CIP catalogue record for this book is available
from the British Library.

ISBN 0 7496 6579 3 (hbk)
ISBN 0 7496 6586 6 (pbk)

Series Editor: Jackie Hamley
Series Advisor: Dr Barrie Wade
Series Designer: Peter Scoulding

Printed in China

The Nightingale

Retold by Anne Cassidy

Illustrated by Serena Curmi

W

FRANKLIN WATTS

LONDON•SYDNEY

Once upon a time,
a nightingale came to stay
near the Emperor's palace.

The nightingale sang the most beautiful song in the world.

One day, a servant brought the nightingale into the palace, so that the Emperor could hear her sing.

"How sweetly she sings!"
everyone said.

The Emperor was so
happy, he cried.

"Please take this present,
dear nightingale!" he said.

But the nightingale shook
her head. "Your tears are
enough for me, Emperor."

Soon, everyone knew how much the Emperor loved the nightingale's song.

Then a present arrived –
a mechanical nightingale,
covered in jewels.

From Japan

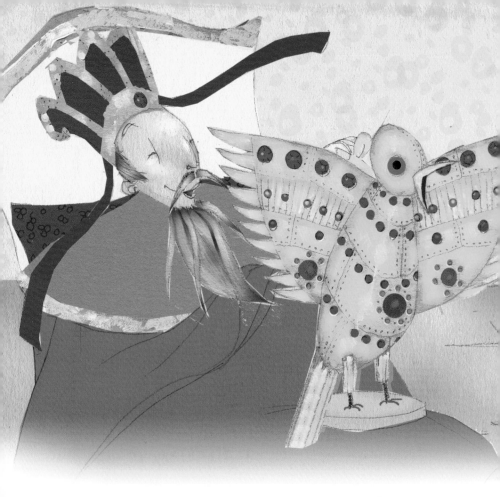

The Emperor wound it up
and it sang a lovely song.
It sang its song over and
over again.

"The mechanical nightingale
is so much prettier than
the real nightingale,"
everyone agreed.

The mechanical nightingale
sat by the Emperor's bed,
singing the same song
again and again.

The real
nightingale
flew away.

Then, one day, the mechanical nightingale stopped singing.

The watchmaker fixed it, but warned: "You can only play it once every year!"

Some years later, the
Emperor lay ill in bed.
"I need music!" he said.

But the mechanical
nightingale was quiet.

Everyone was sad. They thought that the Emperor would never get better.

23

Then the Emperor heard
a beautiful song. It was
the real nightingale.

24

25

"Thank you for coming back, dear nightingale," said the Emperor.

He pointed to the
mechanical nightingale.
"Smash it up!" he cried.

"No!" said the nightingale. "Keep it, and I'll come and sing for you sometimes."

The Emperor soon got better. But the nightingale still comes to sing for him.

Leapfrog has been specially designed to fit the requirements of the National Literacy Strategy. It offers real books for beginning readers by top authors and illustrators.

There are 49 Leapfrog stories to choose from:

* hardback